ONE:

Mary-Sue

Mary-Sue had always felt like she was meant for something more.

Mary-Sue was indisputably the most beautiful woman in the world. 18 years of age, she was quite tall at 6'11. Her long neon-pink hair cascaded in waves over her broad powerful shoulders. When she stood, its curly volume would fall all the way to her feet; however, currently she was sitting at her large glass desk and was letting it pool out over the floor. Her hair never seemed to get dirty or fall out of place and she never bothered with it or cut it, and, of course, she was far too agile to let it trip her.

Her supremely strong, yet feminine, body was the envy of every man and woman in the world. She was perfectly proportioned. Her flawless porcelain skin looked soft to the touch, but was hard all over her body, every muscle taut and tight like a wound spring. Her only blemish was a birthmark in the shape of a heart over one eye, which only served to make her more interesting to look at. Her measurements were 38L-22-40 and when she moved it was sexy poetry in motion. The way her breast jiggled and her hips swayed as she walked on her long toned legs caused men and women alike to be unable to think or do anything other than watch and want.

Her panther-like body was not as striking as her face, however. Her nose was perfect; her lashes naturally long and thick. Her silvery shining eyes, which changed color based on her mood, had a way of boring into a person's soul. Currently, while she was lost in

1

thought, they were a deep ocean blue. When she looked at someone with those vibrant orbs that person knew that she was the only thing that mattered. She was so special and superior that simply having her acknowledging someone else was enough for them to be eternally grateful.

She had hired makeup artists from all over the world to try and enhance her natural beauty, but all had failed. Many of the famous makeup artists, who had worked on so many supermodels, would find themselves staring with wanton awe into her perfect beauty. So overcome by what they saw in her wise intelligent eyes that they would be unable to finish and would just start to gaze into them, forever lost. Luckily she found that, even when expertly applied, makeup only served to cover up her dazzling countenance and her perfect face was only lessened by its presence. Her full lips needed no color other than their natural ruby red. Her eyes could not be highlighted. Mary-Sue felt it was terribly hard being so pretty since so many people could not fully handle being near her spender. Only the strong of will could see her and not be lost to her.

But, Mary-Sue had always felt like some part of her was missing.

In her free time, like today, Mary-Sue would go back over the events of her life to try and find out what. She was currently sitting in her office at the top floor of the largest building in New York. She was a trillionaire and CEO of the world's largest company, a company she herself had found 2 years ago. Her life had not always been like this. People always said her smell reminded them of happy childhood memories, but to Mary-Sue she had no smell. It might be because Mary-Sue had no happy childhood memories.

She had been born in abject poverty as an only child to a loving family. She could not remember much about her father and mother, since they had both died when she was very young. For some reason she had always felt responsible for their deaths. Her whole young life she could remember had been nothing but misery. Bounced from foster home to foster home, Mary-Sue remembered being unwanted and alone. She felt that was why she was unable to form a real bond with anyone; well that, and the fact she knew she was so much better than everyone now, but this had not always been true.

As a child, Mary-Sue remembered being quite plain and not sticking out in anyway. Since she moved around so much she remembered always being the newcomer, the outsider. She remembered her grades were bad and none of her foster parents loved her and were always trying to get rid of her.

This had all changed around the age of 13. She had quickly developed into the prefect woman she now was. Her eyes and hair hand changed color and she started getting straight A's in everything, even gym. Suddenly, all of the girls that she remembered making fun of her plain looks were threatened and jealous of her perfect beauty. The boys that teased her and scorned her suddenly all wanted her and fell over each other trying to help her or impress her.
Not that she needed anyone's help anymore.

Later, she had tracked all of her classmates down and had broken each and everyone one of them. They all were now her personal servants, completely enamored with her, and they all felt deep shame for the way they had treated her.

She had quickly grown taller and stronger as well as prettier and smarter. She joined the school's football and wrestling teams at age 14 and was the star of both. She could easily out-perform all of the boys and, unprecedentedly, after rigorous drug testing, she was recruited by the NFL at age 15. People flocked to the stands to see this stunningly pretty pink haired 15-year-old girl compete with men almost twice her age. Not only did she compete, she won player of the year on her 16th birthday, the same year she quit to found her own company. While she had been playing for the NFL she had used some of the money they gave her in endorsements to enroll in 3 different online PhD programs from major universities, and had completed all in under a year. Earning doctorates in Finance, Marketing, and Theoretical Physics. She did not really need the last one but had found the subject matter interesting.

Her company's chief product was herself. She had realized that she made more on sponsors than she ever did playing for the NFL. Her foster parents had tried to get their hands on her money, but passing the bar and representing herself, she had won the court case and had become legally an adult. Her foster parents were now the janitors of this very building, not able to find any other jobs after Mary-Sue had blackballed them.

With her newly formed company, she had originally charged money to use her likeness on products. But, as she grew more and more alluring as she aged, she started to also demand royalties on every unit sold with her face. Other companies had laughed at that idea, but the soon found they could not be competitive if they did not. Mary-Sue's fans had become so numerous and her face was so captivating people requested it on all their products. When she had reached 17 years of age she had become so breathtakingly beautiful no one, man or woman, could resist her. She was able to charge more and more for the use of her image and companies were forced to pay or go out of business. Soon people realized that Mary-Sue had a lawful monopoly on the one thing in the world that truly mattered, herself. Currently 90% of everything sold in the world had her face somewhere on it, and the other 10% was either going bankrupt or about to cave to her demands.

Her company also made products of its own. Mary-Sue was a master baker and she had evolved a cookie so delicious that the FDA had originally banned it assuming some form of addictive drug was an ingredient. However, they were wrong; Mary-Sue just had figured out the optimal mix of mundane spices to create the perfect baked good. She had to bake a batch in front of a committee to win that legal battle, but now "Mary-Sues" were sold all over the world. It was said that people would rather starve if they could not get their Mary-Sues. The fact that the box was plastered with her face also helped sales.

Mary-Sue's company had also branched into other things. After getting an advance degree in computer engineering she had created a video game with the most powerfull AI known to man. The military was still trying to figure out its coding. Mary-Sue had promised that if anyone could beat the final boss on the most difficult setting, they could play Mary-Sue in real life. Mary-Sue hardly ever did live appearances at that point, so the prize was highly sought after. Months after the release, a South Korean had finally won it. He played Mary-Sue after that in 20 strait games. Mary-Sue had won every one, even after she had been given a handicap. The contest winner was in a state of shock after he lost, but said he learned more about how to play in those few hours than he had in the months before.

Mary-Sue did every so often appear in pubic. She was an accomplished musician and would occasionally do concerts. The ticket prices were obscene, but people would fight each other to go. Scalping never happened at one of her concerts since no one would ever give up a ticket once they got it. No recording devices were allowed on the premises, and Mary-Sue had written a computer virus that would destroy any recording of her voice found online.

At these concerts Mary-Sue would play an instrument of her own invention, and would sing. She had written a single song called "The One True Song." She rarely preformed it anymore because people were never the same after hearing it. They would claim that after hearing her song nothing in life could even come close in comparison. For those people, it was as if all the color had left the world. Like they had felt true happiness once and could never feel it again.

Music critics quit their jobs after attending, unable to find joy in any other music; as if everything else was a pale imitation of The One True Song they had heard. Hearing Mary-Sue sing was said to be a death sentence; even if you did not kill yourself, as many did after, it was like you died on the inside. It was so lovely you would live your life trying to get back that feeling you had lost and never being able to. Once she had let someone record and continue to listen to the song to see if they could live a normal life. They could not. Their body used up all of its endorphins, but that did not seem to matter to them, the song stimulating the pleasure centers of the brain directly. However, the person's mind had quickly broken, delight had turned into delirium and then into a smiling coma-like state they had never woken from.

Now, Mary-Sue mainly played for the terminally ill, who would almost always end up leaving her everything when they did die, so grateful they were for the chance to hear The One True Song before they passed.

Because of all this, and how intelligently she had invested all of the money she made, Mary-Sue was phenomenally wealthy. She, personally, was now making a little under 5 trillion dollars a year. Her company was well over 60% of the world's economy, and that number was only going up.

But, Mary-Sue had always felt like something important was incomplete in her life.

Mary-Sue felt like everything she did was to fill the gnawing hole in her life, and none of it did. She sat in her office in the largest building in the world at the age of 18 wearing a pink striped business suit that had been made explicitly to show off her perfect curves. Everything in her office was made of a clear glass crystal. She could look down onto Times Square and all she saw looking back was pictures of her own perfect face. Every billboard, every commercial, all of it had Mary-Sue's likeness on it, and all paled next to the real thing.

She stood. In her black stiletto heals, with laces all the way to her knee, she was 7'6. When she stood her servant, who was one of the girls that had been mean to her in school, came over to her with an exotic blend of tea, as she had been trained to do. Steam rose out of the crystal cup as Mary-Sue took one sip then purposefully dropped it on the floor. The expensive liquid, which was worth more than her servant made in a year, spilled out onto the carpet floor. Mary-Sue took one of her splendid and elegant long legs and used her heel to ground the cup into a fine dust. Mary-Sue looked down at her servant passed her own massive jiggling bust, and said in a dangerous voice as her eyes flashed a cool blue, "Don't bring me cold tea again."

The girl knew better than to say anything other than "Yes, of course mistress," and immediately started cleaning up the mess. Her classmate servants had been trained that this kind of treatment was what they deserved after the way they had behaved towards Mary-Sue in school, and they knew never to displease their mistresses.

Mary-Sue moved on her long regal legs over to her office's walk-in closet; her pink hair trailed behind her like a train. Another classmate-turned-servant knew this signified that Mary-Sue meant to go out clubbing tonight. He called down to the front desk to let them know to summon Mary-Sue's 100 Best Friends. Mary-Sue's staff had been highly trained to anticipate her needs and actions. Those that did not, did not last long in her employment, and had difficulty finding a job anywhere afterwards. Mary-Sue was no longer a person anyone would cross, and those that met with her displeasure often found their lives forever ruined. But, people thought that was just because of her rough childhood and the public always forgave her, feeling such actions justified.

This servant's job was also to report to sales when Mary-Sue picked what she was wearing for the evening. They needed to immediately change the price to at least ten times what they were currently asking for the style before Mary-Sue appeared outside wearing it. All stores across the country would be alerted. Whatever Mary-Sue wore would define the newest trend in fashion, and if her own people were too slow in capitalizing on that fact, they would find themselves out of a job.

Mary-Sue disappeared into her closet and quickly reemerged wearing a stunning bright green dress and 8-inch green stiletto heals. The dress looked like it was clinging on to her for dear life, accentuating her curves, legs, butt, and bust. It was sleeveless and shoulder-less, and seemed almost as if it had been glued on. Mary-Sue's servant made the call and soon a new line of dresses called "envy" were in production. No one could look like Mary-Sue did in them, but other women would try to live vicariously.

Mary-Sue made her way to the express elevator were her bodyguards awaited. The elevator would quickly bring her to her private exit. There her pink stretched Hummer was already gassed and ready to go. 100 select people, 50 men and 50 women, would be waiting to come with her in stretched limos. They were the luckily 100 to be counted "Mary-Sue's Best Friends". They had undergone many trials and tests to earn this honor. Additionally, each of them had undergone plastic surgery at Mary-Sue's direction and forsook all other friends and family. Their lives were completely dedicated to being perfect friends for Mary-Sue; nothing else mattered to them.

Roads would be closed for her entourage to reach it's destination. The paparazzi were everywhere. Mary-Sue felt it was very hard to live this way, but she understood that taking such pictures of her were necessary to increasing her stock price. They would never get one of her doing anything embarrassing anyway and she owned all of the tabloids; she had found them to be the prefect propaganda machines.

Mary-Sue instructed the driver where they would be going. As expected, it was to one of the few clubs in the city she did not own, yet. Police escorted them through the city and lights and traffic was diverted to make sure she reached the club in minimum time. When they arrived the manager of the club was outside to greet them. Mary-Sue's long stiletto-clad legs emerged from the vehicle. Then, so did the rest of her. She quickly surveyed the nightclub with her silvery eyes and looked down at the owner who was sweating. He had known this day would come, and knew he could not refuse to sell Mary-Sue his club for whatever she wanted. It had been a long time since anyone had turned down one of Mary-Sue's offers to buy, and it had not ended well for anyone other than Mary-Sue.

Looking at the manager Mary-Sue reached into her massive jiggling bust and withdrew a picture of herself and a pen. In front of the gathering crowed and paparazzi she signed it and handed it to him. A personally signed picture of Mary-Sue was worth more than gold. The owner was ecstatic.

Mary-Sue's bodyguards went into the club to clear it out as her 100 Best Friends got ready to go inside. They had brought their own alcohol, more expressive and intoxicating than anything found anywhere in the city. Still only 18, it was illegal for Mary-Sue to drink in public, so this would be a private party. Mary-Sue's entourage had also brought their own DJ and all of Mary-Sue's favorite songs. One of the CDs even had The One True Song on it; the only such CD known to exist. It was more there as a reminder, however. If this party did not live up to Mary-Sue's expectations, she would play it for them over and over to liven things up, and then get 100 new Best Friends. She had done this twice already.

Mary-Sue's 100 Best Friends went into the club first and got the party started, then Mary-Sue herself walked in. Every part of her body moving in such ways even her Best Friends, who saw her nearly everyday, were completely in awe. She went over to a keg filled with Antarctic Nail Ale. She placed her hands on the keg, grabbed it, and lifted her long perfect legs into the air. Holding onto the keg, she balanced herself. She was upside-down with her powerful arms straight, doing a keg-stand. Four of her strongest

male Best Friends held her mammoth breasts in place so they did not fall into her face while two of her female Best Friends gave her the spout to the keg. Mary-Sue drank and drank, upside down, her friends working the pump, until the keg was completely empty.
She delicately set herself down on her green 8-inch heels and let out an unladylike belch, which smelled of sunny summer days. She then nonchalantly walked over to the VIP area were many of her friends were already pouring her shots of 160-proof rum. They all knew that she would be challenging them to a drink off. Going shot for shot, they would drink 75- proof whiskey and she would drink the rum, after already drinking a whole keg of ale. They knew that if they did not put up a fight and try their hardest she would know and be displeased.

Mary-Sue lined them up and knocked them down. Groups of five at a time went at her until they were all unconscious and than another fresh group would be brought out. While this was happening, the non-drinking girls and guys were dancing on the dance floor or making pleasant conversation trying to have a great time for Mary-Sue.
The party was really going well. People were dancing and talking and the club was alive with activity. Mary-Sue had gone through 2 groups of men, when suddenly she stopped. Her eyes changing to pink, and putting her glass down, she quickly strode across the noisy room to a corner were two girls were talking.
She stood behind one of them and the room grew silent; the DJ stopped the music. The girl looked more frightened than a deer caught by a wolf. She slowly turned around and cringed when she saw Mary-Sue's pink eyes looking back at her. "What did you say?" Said Mary-Sue in her icy cool voice.
The wide eye's girl started to stammer, "I.. I.. I was just talking about our current president and his economic policy..."
Mary-Sue cut her off, "Yes, I heard your ignorant opinions on how to simulate the economy from across the room. Give me your Best Friend Bracelet."
The girl hung her head in disgrace and removed the gold brace-

let with the letters "MSBF" engraved on it from her wrist. Shame-faced, she handed it to Mary-Sue, stood and walked out of the room. Everyone watched her go. They all knew the punishment for voicing options Mary-Sue did not approve of, and they also knew that girl's life was now effectively over. Like all of them, she had given up everything to be Mary-Sue's Best Friend and now she had nothing. That unique gold bracelet would be given to one of the thousands that were training for the honor of being one of Mary-Sue's Best Friends. Almost everyone felt nothing in the world was more valuable than the right to wear one of those bracelets.

When the girl left, the party resumed. Mary-Sue's Best Friends also knew they had to keep their conversations interesting or Mary-Sue, who was listing to all of them while she drank, would grow bored and play The One True Song. It was a delicate balance to maintain, but they had been extensively trained for just this. Luckily, they knew that soon the second part of the party would soon start.

After Mary-Sue had drank five separate groups under the table, she again stood. After consuming so much alcohol Mary-Sue was indeed intoxicated, but it did not impair her prefect balance. Walking on her stately legs and 8-inch stilettos, she made her way to the center of the dance floor; her hips and breasts swaying. She had to be good and hammered to dance or else the breathtaking sight might kill some of the onlookers. Even impaired as she was, Mary-Sue's Best Friends all braced themselves as the DJ put on one of her favorite dancing songs.

Words cannot describe what followed. Many of the audience passed out from the spectacular sight that assailed them. Today Mary-Sue had made her dance irresistibly seductive. Woman and men alike began to turn into lust filled animals. Their training, nothing, could have prepared them for this, and Mary-Sue knew it. Her Best Friends lost all control of themselves as she moved across the dance floor. Soon, as Mary-Sue had planned, they had no choice but to carry out their wanton desires. Mary-Sue would use up all of them that night. All of them pleasuring her and ravishing her would prove to not be enough, and by the end she was the only one left conscious. She had driven them all into exhaustion, spurring them on to perform more and more for her. By the end, all 100 of them were completely spent trying to please her.

Mary-Sue's dress was in tatters, and she called to her bodyguards, who had been waiting outside, to get her a new one of the same style. She left the nightclub at 6 in the morning, all her Best Friends moaning or unconscious on the ground.

Looking around at them, Mary-Sue could not help feeling her life was meant for so much greater.

It was now Saturday and she was driven home in her pink stretched Hummer. Her mansion was on Park Avenue; she had gutted an entire block to build her 100-story home. It too had been made of glass crystal; she had designed it herself in such way it was only translucent from the inside. When inside the crystal did not even look tinted, but it was completely opaque outside. Her old classmate servants opened the front door for her as she walked inside.

No one was allowed inside this building but Mary-Sue. The perimeter was completely surrounded and she had bought all of the blocks surrounding the building, filling them with her security personal. Helicopters took off and landed around her mansion. Food was delivered to the adjacent building; an elaborate pipe system Mary-Sue designed would bring prepared food to whatever room she would specify from inside. Dirty dishes and clothing was similarly deposed of. There were no phones inside the building and everyone knew they would have no contact with Mary-Sue until Monday. Mary-Sue valued her privacy.

This is why Mary-Sue was dismayed and a little surprised when she took her elevator to her room and found an old man in them. Before Mary-Sue could say anything the man took her by the hands. Ecstatically he said, "Exalted Princess! I am so happy we finally found you. It must have been awful for you living with these primitives and with only one one-thousandth of your true power." Continuing he said, "No matter, now that we have found you, you can finally finish your training and defeat the Faceless One who did this to you."

Hearing that a dazzling smile spread over Mary-Sue's countenance as her eyes changed to a vivid green. "Tell me more," was all she said.

MARY-SUE PART2:

The Three Sues

Mary-Sue was fairly certain the little man before her was insane.

Two things stopped her from forcibly ejecting him from the top of her 100-story Park Avenue glass-crystal mansion. One was that she was interested to learn how he got past her security system. She had designed the system herself and even if all of her guards had been bought off - something she knew could not happen, such was their dedication to her - no man could have gotten into her bedroom without setting off a dozen alarms and then begin torn to pieces by lasers.
The second reason was something she could not put her finger on. Something about this man rang true with her. He was a curiosity. People had stopped truly interesting Mary-Sue long ago; they seemed so simple. For some reason this was not the case with this man. Mary-Sue did not like not knowing something and she wanted to understand this little man before getting rid of him.

The man had been babbling since she got here. "Oh, Exalted Princess... oh, I mean Exalted Empress now. Begging your pardon, it was my distress that caused me to make such a grievous error. This lowly one will submit himself for punishment when we get back, but it's so horrible to see you in such a state. I am shocked these primitives are keeping you in this tiny hut. Even your lowly servants would not be forced to live lower than the 150th floor of your planet place. To see your splendor shoved into this hovel? Outrageous! And your clothes? To see you in such ghastly rags brings tears to my eyes! I can't believe how these hairless apes are mistreating you. To find you like this is appalling. We will..."

Mary-Sue, whose clothes were worth more than a middle class family made in a year, was a little insulted by all this, her eyes turning a light yellow. "Who are you?" She said in a commanding tone cutting off his ranting. Despite her long night she decided she wanted a drink. Walking over on her long, stiletto-clad legs to her personal liquor cabinet, she poured herself some Navy strength gin. Her prefect body moving in a way she knew would get any man's attention. Her eyes turned a deeper yellow when this man did not even seem to notice.

"Oh, Exalted Empress, the rumors were true then? The Faceless One did not just de-power you and exile you, it violated your mind as well? AND these savages have you pouring your own drinks?" This seemed to be too much for the little man who broke down crying.

At this point in the conversation Mary-Sue realized that he was taking in a faster cadence than a human should be able to. To a normal human the sounds he was making would be an indistinguishable buzz as one word bled into the next. Additionally, he was speaking American English but with no regional accent Mary-Sue could distinguish, and she knew she knew them all. Another curiosity about the man, even his clothing was nondescript. Mary-Sue could often tell a person's whole life history just from watching and listening to them for a few minutes, but she was getting nothing from this man. She had to admit, it was all very intriguing.

Mary-Sue's eyes changed to purple and she decided to pour the man a drink from her private wine collection, hoping it might calm him. She opened a bottle of Shipwrecked 1907 Heidsieck and poured him a glass. She walked over and handed it to him.

He looked shocked, "Exalted Empress! You should not be sullying your exquisite hands by pouring the likes of me a drink, but, oh

Perfect One, bless you."

Taking the crystal cup he tasted the priceless Champagne. Making a face he looked almost as if he would wretch. "These monkeys are forcing you to subsists on this weak tasteless swill? Oh, Flawless One, I must take you away from here! This insipid planet is no place for your radiance. They're simple understanding cannot appreciate you for what you are!"

Mary-Sue realized that she would actually have to really ask this man some questions if she wanted to get any information out of him. She was so used to just knowing everything she needed to know, and having others just know what was expected of them or get fired, it was a little frustrating. As she became frustrated her eyes changed to a light orange, and she was about to speak, but as her eyes changed the man said: "Oh, Exalted Empress, please don't be frustrated with your humble servant. I have been neglect in my duties. The pain of seeing you so mistreated addled my wits for a moment. This lowly one will submit himself for punishment later, but first let this worthless one explain to Your Perfection who you are. It is clear the Faceless One took your memories. They told me this might have happened and that I should be prepared to explain everything to you, even though, of course, it is truly no one's place to explain anything to the Empress of the Universe Made Whole."

Mary-Sue knew who she was and was more interested in knowing who he was, but decided to let the man speak. She was loath to ask people questions about themselves anyway. Her eyes changed back to their neutral silver and she sat down in one of the big chairs that adorned her room. She crossed her perfect legs. Swilling the gin in one hand, she indicated with the other she would listen to his story.

The man seemed to understand. Nodding he collected himself and began.

"For untold eons the universe was divided almost evenly into the two great superpowers. One empire was the Philosphites. Their kingdom was founded on the principle of reason and the advancement of science. No more technologically advanced people ever existed. They could create stars and wormholes. They tamed the heavens with their intellect. Their Emperors were genetically altered to be the smartest creatures in the universe; their brains more powerful than any computer could hope to be. Each Emperor's brilliance eclipsed the last, for the only thing the Philosphites truly valued was intelligence. Because of this they were a delicate people, needing devices even to do something as simple as move.

"The other vast empire was the Amazinines. Their empire was founded on the principle of honor and strength. They had no need of technology to travel to distant worlds, for they possessed the power of flight. On mighty wings they could propel themselves to the upper atmosphere and then, using biological processes, even traverse the cosmos faster than light. Their bodies adapted to space as they used the very radiation of the stars as food. Their DNA was so intricate that not even the Philosphites could unravel its secrets. Selective breeding made their Queen the pinnacle of physical perfection. Her senses heightened beyond even those of other Amazinines, who could already see for light-years. She was impervious to anything less than a hyper-nova, and strong enough to fly through planets. She needed to be that strong, for the only thing the Amazinines truly respected was strength.

"As you can imagine, there was constant strife and war between these two great empires. Whole solar systems were destroyed as these powers clashed. The stars themselves were used as weapons of war. Common ground could not be found between them. The Philosphites could not respect the Amazinines and the Amazinines could not respect the Philosphites. But, amongst the chaos, a solution was found by a third party.

"You see, in all of the infinite cosmos there was only one planet that was able to harness the power of Magic: the Planet of the

Gem. The citizens of that planet called themselves the People of the Gem and using their skill, which was neither physical nor technological, they could cause their planet to disappear from all the scans of the Philosphites, as well as the heightened senses of the Amazinines. They made it move about the cosmos at will. While almost all planets of note were either allied with the Amazinines or the Philosphites, the Planet of the Gem was totally independent. From all worlds and all races they would find any child that held the gift of Magic, though few from the actual races of the Amazinines or the Philosphites, for they both make poor Mages. They would take these protégés and teach them in their secret ways. I was one such child."

Mary-Sue interrupted at this point, her eyes changed to a light pink. He balked at her eye change, and prostrated himself before her. Mary-Sue said, with an edge in her voice, "You're telling me you're a... wizard?" She had half a mind to throw him out at that.

The little man started to grovel. "Most Enlightened One, I beg your forgiveness. I am more of a seer. But, I am first and foremost your servant. Please," he said spreading his hands in a pleading gesture, "for my sake allow me to continue."

This was not how Mary-Sue had planned to spend her weekend. She sighed. Her eyes changed back to their neutral silver and she waved her hand. She was beginning to realize that this man could sense her mood better than even one of her highly trained servants. As she suspected, he understood that she meant for him to continue without her having to say it.

"I was one of most gifted Seers of the People of the Gem. It was I," he said, not without some pride, "that foresaw that, in the end of the war between the Amazinines and the Philosphites, the Universe itself would be consumed. Thus, the People of the Gem could no longer remain neutral; we had to act to end the war with lasting peace instead of ultimate destruction. I lead the seers in trying to find a way towards peace, and it was in my seeing pools that I first saw you, oh Perfect One. You, Merry-Melody-Solemnity-Twilight-Resplendence-Theresa-Sumptuous-Suzanne, First of Her Name and Princess of the Universe Made Whole.

The man understood that Mary-Sue wanted him to stop again, before she even started to raise her hand to indicate she did. When he stopped Mary-Sue said, "I will only allow you to continue if you never mention that stupid name again."

The man seemed to not to know what you say. "But Your Excellency, you loved..."
"Refer to me as Mary-Sue in the story from now on." Mary-Sue said sharply. The man nodded and continued.

"I was the first to ever view your perfection. In all of the timelines and all of the infinite outcomes I saw, there was only one in which such an unequaled individual existed, and it was the only one in which the universe found the Forever Peace I was searching for."

He paused and looked Mary-Sue in her silvery eyes. "I am reputed to be the greatest seer to ever live, and I can assure you, Merry... umm... Sue, that not only are you the most perfect being in the entire universe, you are also the most perfect being in all possible universes. When I saw you in the sea of possibilities, I knew it was my duty to do everything in my power to actualize and aid you. I count myself first among your many servants because I was the first to understand it is everything's purpose to serve only you. Only when all living things worship your perfection will the universe find the Forever Peace."

Mary-Sue was used to complements, but even she was a little flattered by that one. Especially because, based on his pulse and tone, she could tell he completely believed what he was saying. Her eyes became slightly blush.

"I brought my findings to the other members of the Counsel of 14." The man seemed to sense Mary-Sue's confusion at that and quickly explained. "Each of the Schools of Magic had a head member, I was the head of the 14th school, the Seer's School." Again the man seemed to know what Mary-Sue was thinking and continued quickly.

"When I showed your splendid image to the Counsel and explained the ramifications of your existence they were all in complete agreement with me. We knew we must do all within our power to make sure you were born, and that there were only two people in all of the universe that could be your mother and father: The Emperor of the Philosphites and the Queen of the Amazinines.

"Working together we knew we of the Council could make your parents fall in love, and stay in love. The Philosphites might never be able to respect the stubborn Amazinines but they respected their Emperor, and the Amazinines could never respect the fragile Philosphites, but they respected their Queen. We of the Council manipulated events so the two would meet. Not an easy task since, while the Amazinic Queen was always in the thick of the battles, the Philosphic Emperor was always far from the front line. However, the Council of 14 was skilled in manipulation and the meeting took place. Our enchantress made your parents fall helplessly and permanently in love, which temporarily ended the war.

"But, we all knew that as soon as your parents died the war would resume. This is why you needed to be born. It is against the very laws of nature for an Amazinines and a Philosphites to conceive a child together, and our biomancer was very adept at breaking the laws of nature. We could have gotten your parents to conceive you without them even knowing we had tampered, but we wanted to take a more active role in your raising. There were things only we must teach you, and we needed time to make you perfect. We planted the idea of a child your parents' heads, and waited for them to seek us out. They had no idea of our involvement up to this point, although both knew of our existence.

"Your parents went on a epic quest together to locate us, not knowing we had been watching them all along. Finally they found us and beseeched our aid. We, of course, agreed to help them conceive you, on the condition that we could help raise you as well. Because of our neutrality in the war, they agreed. All 14 of us assisted our biomancer in your conception. We needed to make sure you had all of the best qualities of both your parents. You needed to be the pinnacle of both great races. We also gave you other secret abilities, one from each of the 14 Schools of Magic.

"When you were born it was clear we had succeeded. You survived the riggers of an Amazinic birth, which proved you were already stronger than any other species in the universe. When you were delivered you could already speak 27 languages, having learned them by listening in the womb. Your father only knew 11 when he was begot. Additionally, thanks to our magic, you were the prettiest example of either species; your wings angelic. Anything gazing upon you would instinctually know you were their superior. Everything that saw you would want nothing more than to serve you. You would be the prefect leader I had foreseen"

The man saw that Mary-Sue had a question and stopped. Mary-Sue's eyes were a deep purple. "Are you saying that when I was born I was already better than any human?" Something that had always galled her was that she was such an ordinary child. It was only at the age of 13 that she had become special. She found herself wanting deep in her heart to believe what this man was saying about her birth.

The seer looked a little confused at her question. "Mistresses, forgive my ignorance, but I am not sure what you're asking. Are you asking if you, Merry... um... Sue First of Her Name and Empress of the Universe Made Whole, were born better than... than these hairless monkeys that roll around on this ball of dirty iron they call a planet?" He seemed very confused, "To even voice that the two could be compared... why, it would be death on some planets... Why would you..." He paused and then, suddenly, his eyes went wide in horrific realization.

"Exalted Empress, the Faceless One, it... it did not just take your memories, did it? It... gave... you... new ones... It..." His hands when to his face as if he was trying hold back the words. "It **mind raped** you, and... and... no... it couldn't've." His face was pale.

"What?" Mary-Sue said a little surprised at the man's reaction to her question.
"It..." and the worlds came tumbling out of the man. "It made you think you were *human*? An animal? That you were born one of these..." He was uncontrollably crying now, unable to finish.

Mary-Sue contemplated getting out of her chair to comfort him, but decided against it. She did resolve to listen to the rest of this ridiculous story, however. She was convinced this man was completely insane, but she found herself enjoying what he was saying. Something about this fantastical tale was resonating with her. *And I still need to find out how he got in here*, she thought. When he was done crying she told him to continue. It looked like he wanted to do something else, but he followed her orders.

"Even at a young age you were stronger than your mother, smarter than your father and, of course, your beauty was without equal. Everyone loved you. Because of your perfect intelligence, unsurpassed strength, and physical invulnerability, both the Amazinines and the Philosphites acknowledged you as the rightful heir to both empires."

"But," Mary-Sue asked, "would not the war resume upon my death?"

The seer blinked a little when she asked that. "That is unthinkable, Your Highness, you are perfectly ageless, one of the gifts of the Council."

He continued: "Despite your abilities you were such a humble child, and selfless. You never failed to turn a complement back on the one complementing you. Your empathy was without equal and you had many pets; a dragon, 2 flying unicorns, a sphinxe, an ophiotaurus and even the Eplomenicus. You also understood your responsibilities and, while you often wished someone else could shoulder your burden, you understood none could."

Mary-Sue listened to this man tell her about this naive princess who was a stranger to her. This kid sounded nothing like the Mary-Sue she was. Like everything else, animals did like Mary-Sue, but she was more fond of eating them then having them as pets. And, she was nowhere near selfless. Her childhood had taught her to look out for herself since no one else would. As for modesty, Mary-Sue had learned at a young age humility was pointless, especially if you really were the best.

The man continued telling about this perfect little angelic child that was good at everything at such a young age. How she had revived the ancient outdated art of axe-play, how she had found the axe of some great Amazinic prince that could cleave suns in half.

Mary-Sue had mixed feelings about this little girl she was suppose to have been. While the childhood she remembered was hard and bitter, she had grown up hard and resolved because of it. This other girl, despite her abilities, seemed helplessly naive.

When the man started to talk about her Magical training she stopped him again. "You said Amazinines and Philosphites made poor mages." Mary-Sue reminded him, hoping if she caught him in a contraction she could prove to herself he was crazy.
"Oh, yes, most Perfect One, they are." He replied. "Two things are important to a mage. One must have understanding of spells, and one must have the power to cast them. A Philosphite mage knows a great number of spells and has a deep understanding of how they work, but the power to cast them comes from his body, which is frail. Likewise an Amazinic mage has a great amount of power at

her disposal, but little skill or understanding in welding it.

"However, you were the perfect mage. Your mind and body were both tireless. You quickly grasped how a spell worked, and had great inborn power at your disposal. You also invented new spells all the time, something it takes years for a normal mage to do. At last count you had created 572 new spells, 217 of which only the most skilled mages could hope to use, and 42 of which only you could cast because of the power needed and the complexity. You..."

Mary-Sue cut him off again, "Why don't you get to the part about the Faceless One? If I am what you say how did I come here to Earth?"

The man said, "Oh, yes, of course, Most Excellent of All Things, I just love talking about your accomplishments so much. It's a more pleasant topic than the Faceless One's betrayal. But, sadly, you must hear what was done to you." His eyes started to tear up again as he continued.

"We of the Council decided that we needed to make sure your future was secure. We, the People of the Gem, decided you be given the Gem on your 13th name day.

The Gem was our most powerful artifact. It was said that all Magic came from it, and it was buried deep in the heart of our planet. We had brought it to the surface. With the Gem you would no longer just be the heir to the Amazinic and Philosphite empires you would be the rightful ruler of the People of the Gem as well. You would preside over the Universe Made Whole, and, being immortal, you would eternally rule. The Forever Peace I foresaw would begin.

"The Council, after much debate, ruled that they would each put their own life-force into the Gem, imbuing its wear with their wisdom and power. You begged us not to, but our minds were made up. We needed to make sure that you had the power and wisdom to rule the universe for all time.

"On your 13th name day we begin the ritual. It was held on a planet between the Amazinic and Philosphite empires. Your parents were in attendance. We had also decided to link your life-force to that of the Gem. If you were to die, it would be destroyed so no others could have its power. You were brought to that neutral place and, with your own help, we placed you in stasis so we could safely connect your life-force to the Gem. We could only place you in stasis without your wings and depowered, such was your strength even at age 13.

"While you were held we magically removed your wings and started the process. Each Council member in turn gave up his or her skill and power into the Gem. However - and I can only blame myself for this - I did not foresee the 13th Council member, the Faceless One, and its betrayal. The Faceless One was really more of its title, for no one knows its true name, or gender, or race, or, well, anything. The 13th School was that of illusion, and the Faceless One was the most powerful illusionist in our history. It had the power even to cloud my divination. Thus, I was unable to anticipate that after the 12th Council member was absorbed into the Gem, the Faceless One struck. Your parents and I were helpless as it stole what was rightfully yours. Knowing we could not stop the Faceless One while it held the Gem, your parents ordered me back to the Planet of the Gem to try and gather other mages to help. I am something of a gifted teleporter as well as seer. I begged them to come with me, but they stayed to fight a hopeless battle to save you.

"When I got back with reinforcements, I found the whole system decimated. The sun had gone hyper-nova and not even your mother could have survived that. There was no sign of you or the Faceless One, only your angelic wings drifting in the void. I thought the Forever Peace was lost to us. Worse still, I feared the Faceless One had killed you. Not knowing what else to do we went back to our planet.

"Soon however, we learned the Faceless One was masquerading as you. It had the Gem, which meant you must still be alive somewhere, and was ruling both great kingdoms. But, the Faceless One's magic can only fool the Amazinines and Philosphites for so long. It does not have your strength or your knowledge. The Universe is at peace under this usurped rule, but it is not the Forever Peace.

"After 5 years of searching, I have pierced the Faceless One's illusions and found you. I see the Faceless One signed its handy work and left its mark upon you." The little man pointed towards the heart-shaped mark over Mary-Sue's left eye.

He continued, "Exalted Empress, you must come to the Planet of the Gem. You must undo what the Faceless One has done."

There was a pause as he finished his plea. Mary-Sue's eyes remand their neutral silver as she looked at this little man, weighing his worth. Finally, after a long silence, she spoke, "So, what, you'll just teleport me there then?"
The little man nodded, "With your consent."
Mary-Sue let out a musical chuckle at that. "By all means then, teleport away."

However, as soon as she spoke the words she found herself, and the little seer, no longer in her glass-crystal mansion, but on a crystal planet. For the first time in 5 years, Mary-Sue felt true surprise, her eyes changing to a bright gold yellow. What she saw was indescribably beautiful.

The planet's sun was pure white and its surface was a giant prism. Every color could be seen sparking. Rainbows flashed everywhere and, had Mary-Sue been human, the dazing brilliance of it all would have blinded her. Even so it was hard for her to look at anything for too long. Also, she could see deep within the core of the clear planet's crust.

The little seer, who was clearly used to all this, took her by the hand. "Please, Exalted Empress, we must restore your racial heritage first."

"Ummm..." said Mary-Sue, in disbelief for a moment that everything the man said was no doubt true. But she regained herself quickly, her eyes changing back to silver. "How long will that take?"

"Not long at all, oh Perfect One. We suspected that the reason you have not tried to contact us was because of the Faceless One's tampering and are prepared. We can restore your power, but not your memories." He had a great sadness on his face when he said that. "Only the Faceless One itself can do that. You must confront it to get your childhood back." Mary-Sue just nodded.

The man led her into a building that was more spectacular than anything she had ever seen. The hues from each prismatic hill and rise seemed as if they were being channeled into it. It looked as if it was constructed exclusively from multicolored light. Her own mansion was nothing compared to this elegance.

"I am so sorry," said the man, "I wish we had time to clean up for your arrival. But, please, Perfect Empress, forgive this run down place's appearance and, come with me, we are ready for you."

She followed him though unimaginable many-colored crystal beauty until she was in a large rainbow room. Above her she saw 14 huge chairs each a different color. 12 of the chairs were filled with more people like the man that escorted her. However, what really caught her attention was at the center of the room where the colors of each of the chairs converged. There at the center was a pair of silvery-white angel wings. They hung suspended as if under their own power, and even in this room of light, they glowed brighter still with an inner white light. They were the fairest object she had seen in this magical place.

The seer left her side and went to the last of the chairs in the great room. All but one was now filled. Mary-Sue guessed that these must be the new Council members, the 13th black chair left vacant. Mary-Sue could feel the members watching her. She had not felt so small in 5 years. She wondered if they were convinced who she was, but no one said anything. Mary-Sue continued to stare at the wings in the center of the room. Not knowing what else to do, started walking towards them. As she did, a chant rose up from the people in the chairs. She felt like she was moving in a dream. The closer she got to them the more unreal everything felt. Finally, she was close enough to reach out and touch them, so she did. Something miraculous happened.

The feeling was indescribable, Mary-Sue was sure any human would have been instantly destroyed by the sensation. The chanting grew louder and louder, but soon she realized it was her hearing that was improving. Soon she could hear other conversations happening all over the planet. Every vibration of sound in the atmosphere came to her powerful ears. Her eyes also became stronger and stronger. She could see through the walls, through the building, through the planet. She found herself gazing into the sky for light-years. Nothing was hidden. She could hear, see, smell, even feel everything.

The sensations were so great that Mary-Sue was sure even her powerful mind would be overwhelmed, but it was not. It was starting to process all of the information at faster than light speed. Mary-Sue was understanding perfectly everything she was seeing and hearing. She found herself scanning this world as the Council members chanted. She was reading books in libraries at light-speed on the other side of the planet, and everything was making perfect sense to her. All of the information, everything this place had to offer she was absorbing; mastering it and improving upon it.

When she was done with all of the archives on the planet, which seemed to take her only half a heartbeat, she turned her perfect senses onto herself. She could see her skin hardening; her muscles growing and becoming superhuman. She could see her magically enhanced Amazinine-Philosphite DNA asserting itself. She realized that nothing could break her perfect skin now; she could fly into a star with her angelic wings and not even feel it. Not even a hypernova could hurt her in the slightest. Her strength? God-like. She could annihilate planets and move suns.

And her beauty? A crystal planet with the sun hitting it just right was nothing compared to Mary-Sue now. Men and women alike would die within her splendor. Her looks before were superior in every way to every human, and now they were magnified. Her angelic wings glowed. Her vibrant pink hair took on an unearthly quality to it. People would kill each other just for a chance to touch her porcelain skin and long legs. Her beasts made all those that looked upon those joyful orbs weep in pleasure and want. They jiggled in a way to hypnotize and break the strongest of wills.

But, her silvery eyes were her most striking feature. They held power unimagined. Bottomless pits in which everything was lost. She could stare into your soul as you begged her to take your darkest secrets.

Mary-Sue started a sultry laugh. The sound was honorably joyous and wonderfully frightening. It shook the very foundations of the building. Earthquakes rocked the planet itself. She rose into the air, looking down on this oh so fragile world.

The Council members had stopped chanting and started yelling at each other. They could not guess what was happening, but Mary-Sue knew. "She was not this powerful before," one of them cried out.

Mary-Sue just laughed again; the musical, overwhelming sound came from every direction. "Fools," she said in a luscious voice. "I was 13 before, a mere child, not even yet gone through puber-ty. Now, you see before you an Amazinine-Philosphite woman grown; the magically enhanced pinnacle of both."

She raised her hands and the whole planet started to shake again. She knew she could effortlessly destroy them all if she wanted to, but why? It would be a waste. She looked down at them hungrily. She could see their thoughts; their brains working so painfully slow compared to hers. She could watch their synapses firing, and was already figuring out what one nerve or another being active meant.

She laughed again, the noise like rolling thunder. "So, when I am ready I should go fight the Faceless One? This Gem-wielding imposter is meant to be a challenge to me now? I should train and relearn spells and get ready for this battle?"

"Well," stammered the seer, looking up at her, "that was the plan...."

"What can you teach me? I've just read every book and scroll on this planet. I can read the chemical signals in your brain." She looked up to the sky. "I can see a Philosphite computer 4 light-years from here and read the binary stored on it. Oh, it's a quantum computer? I can see the differences in the electron spins. And, in the time it took me to describe all that to you I already processed and fully understood everything in its database. I now know where the usurper is."

Mary-Sue looked back at them. The seer stammered "Well... maybe you should..."

Mary-Sue cut him off, her angelic wings flapping slightly and a creating a gale. "I know the spell used to put the power of the mages into the Gem. I read it on a scroll you have locked away in your deepest vaults. The Faceless One has the power of 12 mages? I can take the power of others as well."

"But... but..." the seer said, "You seem so powerful already... But... why not take me? I will willing give my life for you, my Empress."

"Yes, in fact I bet I could beat the Faceless One right now," Responded Mary-Sue. "But why risk it? I am sure everyone on this planet is like you. They would all give their life for the peace I offer as Empress. I will now use a modified version of that spell, which I just thought of, to absorb every mage on this planet. All of you will give your power to the rightful heir of the Universe Made Whole."

Before anyone else could say anything, Mary-Sue raised her hands and it was done. Every soul on the planet streamed into her. She was ablaze with magical energy. Her skin as white-hot lava. It all happened so fast not a one of them could even scream as they made the ultimate sacrifice for Mary-Sue.

"The Faceless One has 12 mages? Now I have a billion." Mary-Sue said and energy raced over her body and flashed from her eyes. Standing on this dead plane she looked to the sky and flew.

The Faceless One had surrounded itself with an army of both Amazinines and Philosphites, but they were no match for Mary-Sue. She easily destroyed a battalion of Amazinines. They were strong enough to move planets, but she was powerful enough to move suns. Additionally, they could not think as fast as she could. Her body could move faster than light, as could her mind.

The Philosphites' war machines fared no better. She could see every move they wanted to make before they made it. She could easily anticipate everything while reading their computers from light-years away. She quickly and perfectly understood their technology, and thought of hundred of ways to disable it.

More than just defeating them in battle, she was letting them see her. She would pause long enough for those she was fighting to glimpse her in all her glory, their weapons just uselessly bouncing off her indestructible skin. Seeing the face of their true Empress, many were giving up. They saw she was the strongest, and realized she was the smartest. Even with all of its magic, how long could the Faceless One truly pretend to be her, Mary-Sue? 5 years was a long time and Mary-Sue knew the usurper's subjects were already starting to doubt the fake in ways they would never, could never, have doubted her.

Finally, she found her old home, the palace that took up a whole planet. This planet made the Planet of the Gem look homely and crud. 20,000-story golden crystal spires stretched off of the planet's surface. So tall they came into the stratosphere and would need their own atmosphere inside. Statues of Mary-Sue adorned every hing. One statue by the equator was 100 km high; its detail was exquisite, each pink hair was crafted separately. Mary-Sue could see that the statue was made of solid colored platinum and it was ornamented with gems the size of buildings. She paused for a moment to take in all this grandeur while the automated defenses crashed into her sumptuous invulnerable body.

This planet palace was meant for her, but it was occupied by the usurper. She flew to it. The soldiers, both Amazinines and Philosphites had heard she was coming and let her pass. They knew she was their True Empress come back to them. She scanned the planet palace for the Faceless One, as well as for the best way to break in without causing too much damage to her home, and in no time at all she was standing before a duplicate of herself. It looked almost like she had when she was human, except it had a mark in the shape of a heart over both eyes.

When they were together anyone could see it was a pale imitation of the true Mary-Sue. A pale moon reflecting the light of the blazing sun that was Mary-Sue. Before it could do anything she waved her hand and it was held immobile. She waved her hands again, wielding the power of billions of mages, and the simulacrum knelt before her. How anticlimactic, she thought. All too easy.

She looked out at the gathered Amazinines and Philosphites servants.
"Who is your rightful Empress?" she asked, in a voice that shook the heavens and would make angels weep with its melodious resonance.

Without question or hesitation they all knelt before her. "You!" They cried. And with a flick of her wrist the Faceless One disintegrated.

She walked over to where the body had been. "Wow, that really was anticlimactic," she said a little disappointed as she picked up the Gem and put it on her forehead. She already had the knowledge and power of a whole planet of mages, so 12 more was not really that much of an addition. But she took it.
The Gem itself is really pretty, she thought. Then, she realized something. "My childhood memories. I need the Faceless One to give them back to me. I want to remember those spells and where I put that axe." She said to herself as her people crowded around her, all of them crying out how sorry they were for allowing themselves to be deceived by a stupid, weak imposter. Mary-Sue had had enough fawners in her lifetime, and she told them all she needed some time to herself.

As they left to other rooms, she started to look around. This was her true home; her palace. She could see why the seer had called her house on Earth so small. "I could have made my mansion like this in a few more years," Mary-Sue boasted. Then she looked down at the ash that was the Faceless One. "I guess I need you back." She said, and used a forbidden spell one of the mages in the Gem had been working on, and dragged the Faceless One back into the realm of the living.

It still wore her face. She could have pulled that off of it, but she had grown used to seeing her own countenance back on Earth. Indeed, this fake Mary-Sue looked like she had as a human, but the true Mary-Sue was so much more now.
She just looked at it and said, her eyes flashing a dangerous red, "This is not a negotiation. You took my memories and made me forget who I was. You will restore them to me, or I will kill you and revive you a hundred times before I ask you again. After that I will start getting creative … and I can be very creative." She

flashed a smile that would have blinded a human with its brilliance.

The pale silvery eyes of the Faceless One stared into the fiery silver ones of Mary-Sue. Its face twisted into a smile. "I knew you'd come back; I did so ever want to see the monster I created before it all fell apart. Not content and naive anymore are you? I did so enjoy being you for a time, but it only helped a little from the consuming jealousy. Taking everything you had, taking your innocence and complacency, now that did quench my green fires."

Mary-Sue's eyes burned red. She did not bring the Faceless One back to hear its crazy gloating, and she was about to kill it again when it said, "Wait, I'll happily restore your memories." And with a toothy grin that looked out of place on its human Mary-Sue face it brought its hands up to the heart-shaped mark on Mary-Sue. The mark vanished.

Mary-Sue's eyes went wide in shock. She dropped the grinning Faceless One. Mary-Sue's mouth gaped open in realization as her eyes unfocused, "I... kill... my... the People of the Gem... gone... I killed them, they were like my family... and I tortured all those poor human animals." She said in an adorable voice.

"No," another sultry voice came from Mary-Sue as the heart-shaped mark returned, "Who cares about those mages? And my classmates deserved it because of what they did."

"But," the first cute voice said as the mark vanished again, "they didn't do anything, you, I, we... only thought..."

Suddenly, Mary-Sue went still. Her heart-shaped mark flashing. The Faceless One could not help but watch with glee.

Within Mary-Sue a confrontation raged.

With her mind's eye Mary-Sue saw Merry-Melody-Solemnity-Twilight-Resplendence-Theresa-Sumptuous-Suzanne. The little prepubescent princess was dressed in, of all things, a pink tutu.

She was just under 5 feet tall; her angelic wings almost looked glued on and her pink hair fell behind her in long waves. She did not have the heart-shaped mark on her.

Mary-Sue could feel her own heart-shaped mark throb over her left eye. She was in her human body and looked like she had in her office on Earth. Her perfect 38L-22-40 figure hugged by her pink pinstripe business suit. She was, of course, still 6'11", but was closer to 7'5" in heels. Her long black stiletto heels laced up to her knees.

The two pairs of silvery eyes regarded one another. Finally Merry-Melody-Solemnity-Twilight-Resplendence-Theresa-Sumptuous-Suzanne spoke. "You're a selfish bitch." She said in a accusing voice, that could not help but sound adorable.

Mary-Sue almost laughed, and said in sultry voice. "Listen, sister, it's a dog-eat-dog world. I took what was mine because it was offered." Mary-Sue had never realized until now how seductive she sounded when she spoke, but in contrast to her younger self it was clear.

"I am not your sister," Merry-Melody-Solemnity-Twilight-Resplendence-Theresa-Sumptuous-Suzanne said peevishly, but still very cutely. "My sister wouldn't have killed all of those people for power; my sister would not have tortured her human animal classmates because she was insecure about what she thought they did."

Those words of Merry-Melody-Solemnity-Twilight-Resplendence-Theresa-Sumptuous-Suzanne cut Mary-Sue deeply. She felt outrage as her eyes flashed red, "Look here, you're, what, 13? You lived a perfect fairy tale life. How DARE you presume to judge me? I did what I had to do to survive when I was your age, and I came out on top."

"My age?" It was Merry-Melody-Solemnity-Twilight-Resplendence-Theresa-Sumptuous-Suzanne turn to laugh, a sound like a tinkling bell. "You were never my age, you're only 5-years-old."

Mary-Sue let out a tantalizing chuckle. "Does this look like the body of a 5-year-old?" Mary-Sue said alluringly as she traced the voluptuous curves of her body.

"You're a whore." Said Merry-Melody-Solemnity-Twilight-Resplendence-Theresa-Sumptuous-Suzanne bluntly, "and I'll hate you forever."

Mary-Sue was about to retort when Merry-Melody-Solemnity-Twilight-Resplendence-Theresa-Sumptuous-Suzanne opened her perfect little mouth and began to sing. Mary-Sue was surprised that she recognized the song. It sounded like her One True Song, but something was different about it. It was agonizingly sweet. It was so honeyed it hurt to hear. Mary-Sue tried to put her hands to her ears.

She was back in her Amazinine-Philosphite body now in the palace. Mary-Sue could feel Merry-Melody-Solemnity-Twilight-Resplendence-Theresa-Sumptuous-Suzanne still within her, forcing the song from her lips. *That little brat is not stronger than me*, she thought.

The Faceless One, still wearing her face, writhed before her as she sung. Mary-Sue could not stop singing, no matter how much she wanted to. The sound filled the palace, servants fled. They were escaping, but Mary-Sue and the Faceless One's fates were bound together. Blood tricked out of the Faceless Ones ears, and Mary-Sue could feel blood coming from her own. She had to stop singing this song. Her hands flew from her ears to her month, but it was no good. The saccharine song came out of her like syrupy death.

The Faceless One stopped moving. Stronger and stronger the song grew, shaking Mary-Sue to her very core. The only thing that could kill Mary-Sue was Mary-Sue. Blackness and blood closed in around her silvery eyes. Mary-Sue could feel her self slipping away as she sung...

...Darkness...

Then, suddenly, Mary-Sue's silvery eyes opened, but she was still quite dead. She was at the Pearly Gates of Heaven, and she could feel the heart-shaped mark on her left eye.

"Well... fuck," she cursed. Then sighing, "I guess it could be worse." She stood up and dusted herself off, seeing that she was again wearing her pink pinstripe suit and black stilettos. She strode over to the gates on her long perfect legs and was about to open them when a raspy voice stopped her short.

"As a rule," it said, "we don't let genocidal egotists in."

She looked around and saw staring down at her past a huge tome keys in hand was Saint Peter.

MARY-SUE FINAL

Revelations

"Is goodness loved by the gods because it is good, or is it good because it is loved by the gods?"

- SOCRATES TO EUTHYPHRO

The humongous Succubus Queen Mary-Sue lounged idly as she gorged herself on tortured souls. Trillions of them at a time went down her super-hot gullet. They held no calories, adding only power to her fiery form. She was absolutely massive, and only growing. She was completeness and emptiness, salvation through damnation. Her devastatingly flawless legs now seemed to span hundreds of feet, even in Hell where distance held no meaning. Her despoiling hips, breasts, lips, everything about her was overpoweringly seductive and impressive. Her scent, which was more powerful than all of the aphrodisiacs in reality, filled all of Hell. She was an exaggerated example of pure temptation, an oversexed goddess to whom mortals - men and woman alike - would beg to lose their souls. Nothing could resist her, and anything would give her everything without even being asked. Her skin, which used to be porcelain perfection, was now white hot and seemed almost to scorch the eyes to look upon. Her hair also burned a sultry pink in Hell's flickering light, as did her heart-shaped mark. They were symbols of her unquestionable majesty and domination.

With an effortless flick of her dynamic wrist she could destroy even a Prince of the Abyss. She had already demonstrated this the first few times one had challenged her utter supremacy. To serve her was now an unquestionable imperative. Even demons no longer could resist what was she was becoming. With each soul consumed, she grew to be more and more of what she was: Larger than existence; the object of pure untainted lust. Undeniable and unstoppable, after all why should she stop? All that mattered was her. Everything else was so far beneath her as to not warrant notice, and all of reality was slowly learning this simple truth.

Her silvery eyes flashed dangerously as terrified emaciated devils and gaunt demons scurried back and forth bringing her all of the souls within Hell. They all bore her mark and knew that if they displeased her, they would be her next meal ... and they suspected they might be anyway once the damned souls ran out. Mary-Sue was devouring vigintillions of them faster than they were coming in, and no one could guess what she would do when they were all consumed. The denizens of Hell knew this did not matter. They could not deny her anything anymore. On her whim they live and died. Their existence was hers to do with as she pleased, but how could it have come to this, they asked themselves. How indeed.

Before.
Mary-Sue stood outside the gates to Heaven as the Saint with the keys berated her. She let it wash over her, knowing he would pay when the time came, as all that had defied her would. Saint Peter spoke in his rasping voice.
"Heaven is not for the likes of you, but for the humble. You don't even know the meaning of that word anymore."
"What do I have to be humble about?" retorted Mary-Sue. "I am better than everything else. That is not vanity, but a fact."

The Saint scoffed, "See what I mean? Moving on, do you know what's happened to Earth since you left it? Complete social collapse. Everyone is branding that stupid mark over your left eye for themselves to show their support. Many are outside your Park Avenue mansion praying for you to come back to them, but too scared to enter it. It's now a temple to the false idol that is you, Mary-Sue. Also," he continued, "people are killing each other for your stupid cookies that you never bothered to tell anyone else how to make. You made that whole planet completely dependent on you and then you just up and left."

Mary-Sue just rolled her eyes. "So? Why should I care what happens to them? I get to decide who is worthy of my time and who is not."

"Like those billions of mages you absorbed? I mean, we're not exactly fans of magic up here, but, really, billions of souls?"

"They would have gladly given their lives for me. Why don't you ask them," Mary-Sue said confidently.

"Gee," he said sarcastically, "I would, but, you know, you *ate their souls*, so I can't, can I?"

The Saint continued, "That seer should never have seen you in his pools. It was not peace he saw, but the Apocalypse. He was trying to shave off the inevitable, and in so doing clung to an iniquitous path. You were a possibility never meant to become realized; a hybrid that was never meant to be. Your very existence is an affront to the natural order."

"Really," he continued, but this time Mary-Sue felt as if he was talking to someone else; some unseen force. "This whole thing is ridiculous. I mean, I'm the only other character to be given a real name, and not a single character other than Mary-Sue got a proper description this whole time. Everything else is basically described only by its relationship to her, as if she was the only focus. What does a normal Philosphite or Amazinine even look like?" He then seemed to be talking to Mary-Sue again, "Do you know?"

"What?" Mary-Sue felt a little confused all of a sudden; she had no idea what this senile old man was talking about. "Yes, of course I do. A Philosphite is frail and smart and an Amazinine is strong and

THE QUINTESSENTIAL MARY-SUE

has wings."

The Saint laughed." That's all you got? Wings and frailty? Really, what does one *look* like? Heck, what did the seer look like? What was his name? Who were your classmates?"

Mary-Sue did not feel like answering such a stupidly obvious questions.

When she did not respond Saint Peter said smugly, "That's what I thought." Mary-Sue knew she would wipe that insolence out of him.

He continued: "Anyway, in case you did not guess, you're going to Hell. Take that one with you." He pointed behind Mary-Sue and as she turned she saw the Faceless One, still wearing her face, who waved at her impishly.

Suddenly a hole opened in the clouds and Mary-Sue and the Faceless One were falling together.

It was, apparently, a long boring fall from Heaven to Hell.

As they fell the Faceless One would not shut up. Mary-Sue decided she would tolerate its ranting only as long as the purgatory-like fall lasted.

"I did it all for you, you know," the Faceless One was saying as they fell."Merry-Melody-Solemnity-Twilight-Resplendence-Theresa-Sumptuous-Suzanne was always complaining about how difficult her responsibility was. She was always telling me how she wished she did not have the burden. I was jealous of her, of course, but I loved her too. That's the problem with you Mary-Sues," it ranted almost to itself. "Everything must love you, other than authoritative old men, of course.

The Faceless One raved on as Mary-Sue listened stoically.

"I needed to sever your ties with others so that you could be free. I knew the humans would make you callous; that was my plan all along. You see, despite myself, I wanted to make you happy." It explained almost plaintively, "You complained about your responsibility, but I know what the real problem was, your empathy. You cared too much for those around you. You were too close to them. Only wanting to do what was right for them. You burden was not responsibility, but kindness. They raised you to be what they thought was the perfect leader, overloaded with compassion for those under you. But, you did not have to be a pious leader, you just needed to be a leader. A tyrant does not need to care, but under one there still is peace.

"I formed my own plan separate from the naive Council. I could help you by hurting you. It was perfect to feed my jealousy... and my love." The Faceless one said that last part softly, almost as if it meant it.

"You're lying," was all Mary-Sue said.

"Probably." It giggled a little in Mary-Sue's own musical laugh. "It is what I do."

"Why are you still wearing my face anyway, don't you have one of your own?"

"Not really," it said casually, "I even made myself forget who or what I am, makes it easier. But, this is not really your face anyway."

Mary-Sue gave the Faceless One a cold hard stare.

"No really," it said defensively. "Each of the Council members gave you a boon, remember. I was the most powerful illusionist of all time, what do you think my gift was?"

The Faceless One paused dramatically, but when Mary-Sue did not answer, it continued: "It was your looks, of course. The seer thinks he is the first one to have seen your perfection, but actually, it was I. I made your face long ago as the mastery of my craft; the ultimate illusion: perfect flawless beauty. I was actually upset at the seer when he showed your countenance for the first time. I thought that idiot had somehow duplicated my work. But, when he explained everything to us I realized what I was to do. Only I could grant you such loveliness. It was your destiny to be given everything of worth, even my greatest achievement. But we're dead now, so I guess it does not matter."

Mary-Sue just said plainly, "This is only a minor setback. When we get to Hell the first thing I will do is absorb your essence, and

THE QUINTESSENTIAL MARY-SUE

than I will take the place over. It will probably take me a month, tops."

The Faceless One just looked at her, and started to laugh; prettily at first, in Mary-Sue's voice, then with the edge of madness to it.

Mary-Sue had been right about the first part, but wrong about the second. She had eaten the Faceless One's soul first, but it did not take her a month to subjugate Hell; it had taken her less than a week.

Now she was the Succubus Queen of the Damned. The emaciated demons were running out of souls to feed her, but they could not stop. They knew if they slowed for even a second, she would devour them in her gluttony and wrath. She was so immensely powerful now she didn't need them; she just delighted in their servitude. She was created to lead, and she wanted minions under her. Trillions of souls every moment were being fed to her, faster than the wicked were dying. She was insatiable. As she ate, her already immeasurable might grew, as did she her body, a temple to her own pleasure and perfection.

The demons ran around frantically, finding the last few souls in Hell to stuff down her waiting sensual mouth as she reclined on a throne of countless skulls. When they had finally completely exhausted the supply of souls, they threw themselves on the burning ground, begging her. Everything about her now demanded obedience. These demons begged her ... not to spare them, but to give them new orders. Pleading with her to tell them what to do. Should they throw themselves into her mouth next? While non-existence would be horrible because in that state they could no longer serve her, they would prefer it to her going one moment without her desires being fulfilled.

Mary-Sue lazily listened to their pleas. She let them become more and more hysteric and desperate. Without her orders and guidance their demonic lives were unbearable; they need to serve her, to do everything and anything to make her happy. That if she would only notice them again, their existence would be complete. They told her that by not issuing new edicts she was denying them meaning.

At that she laughed, the sound indescribable. In that laugh was all hopes and dreams, all wants and desires. In a voice that brought Hell itself to its knees she said: "Your lives have no meaning. Only I have meaning. Only I matter, and in my ecstasy is your worth. My pleasure your purpose."

All of the demons groveled before her, telling her how correct she was, and how insignificant and trivial they were. But, still, they begged her to punish them for their insolence, to do anything to them.

Again she laughed at their sniveling, the sound overwhelming all with its resonance.

At that, Mary-Sue rose. Flames licked off her and danced around her. Her movements were unhallowed sacred poetry. Salvation and damnation were in each sway of her womanly hips. Each jiggle of her colossal breasts was the epitome of desire, and of need unfulfilled. Reality itself bent to her implacable will as she walked through it.

The citizens of Earth had gathered around Mary-Sue's 100-story crystal mansion, but none had dared go inside. All bore her mark, a heart-shaped burn over their left eye. They implored to her, pleading to her to come back to them. As they prayed a Hellmouth opened around Mary-Sue's block sized mansion. It sunk into the abyss and something even more immensely monstrous came out. As Mary-Sue rose, a cheer came from the gathered crowd. But, crushing awe was soon all they could feel as more of her magnificence came into view. She smelled of burning love mixed with pure lust.

Her hair was like a mistress's whip of pink fire. Her lashes were thick forests of passion. Her silvery eyes seared all souls as she looked at the assemblage, taking what remained of their feeble wills. Her tempestuous lips were hot red rubies, her teeth so bright you felt them leeching the color out of you. Her burning white skin would take more than just your color; it took everything you had. Her stately neck redefined regality.

It seemed to take eternity for her massive mammaries to come fully into view, but as they did the crowd lost it. They were so mammoth they almost did not fit through the block-sized Hell portal. Mary-Sue's bare breasts were everything you had ever wanted and nothing you could ever have, because she had them instead. Her arms were the perfection femininity, but all could see they held the strength of countless souls. With a movement of her long deft hands, she could take anything from anyone -- not that there was need, for every one would gladly give Mary-Sue everything. Her crimson nails were sharp enough to rend reality, but something was so soft and sultry about her perfect fingers. Her abs made diamonds seem like crumbling shale. Her wide flawless hips promised salvation, but gave nothing. Her bottom was the shape of an extra-large sumptuous heart. Her butt was need and desire made fiendish flesh. Her lengthy legs then began to come into view; the pink fire between them was the gate to eternal ecstasy ... and to misery manifest. If it took an eternity for Mary-Sue's tantalizing breasts to rise completely, it was indescribable the time it took her long powerful womanly legs to be fully seen. Pillars of strength and supremacy, they were adorned with the only clothing Mary-Sue now wore: long, red, spiked-stiletto sandal heels, showing off her perfectly painted toes. Her colossal feet were clearly made for stepping on lesser beings, and all beings were her lessers.

Over 100 stories tall, Mary-Sue stood in her full undeniable slendor and dominance. Her pleasure was your pain ... and you'd beg her to dispense it, if only to have her attention for a moment. She was reality's dominatrix.

She barely seemed to notice the gathered multitude as she looked to the stars. Then, in an exquisite moment, Mary-Sue simply took one-third of all that reality had: one-third of the plants, one-third of the water, one-third of the light, and one-third of the lives; all this she took unto herself as trumpets could be heard.

The energy she stole poured into her. What she had been when she entered this plane was nothing compared to what she was becoming. Complete control was hers. The feeling of one-third of all that could have function becoming part of her was ecstasy, unimagined and uncompromisable. She would have taken everything instead of just a third, but it was her wish that her thralls have something left so they could make even more for her

Everything was her slave now. Her image was omnipresent. All art was for her and about her. Paintings, statues, poetry and pose, all of it now created exclusively to venerate Mary-Sue. It could be no other way, since all thoughts were also for Mary-Sue. Dreams and hopes were now only to create something she would take. A person's true aspiration was now to do everything one could to give and give to Mary-Sue's insatiability.

Philosophers pondered questions such as: Could Mary-Sue create a statue of herself even more lovely than herself? The answer was: Of course she could, but she would also still be lovelier than it.

Mary-Sue was all-powerful, so she did not need to have slaves, but it was her desire to be the object of desire and her desire was all that mattered. Across reality children were being taught that it was the meaning of life to work themselves to death creating joy for Mary-Sue and that, in death, their souls would fuel her glory. Obedience to Mary-Sue was not a question, but the ultimate answer.

This was now the purpose of all reality: to add to what she had. Energy, material wealth, pleasure and power, created only to be given as sacrifice to Mary-Sue. All creatures: demons, Philosphites, Amazinines, humans and all others, would work together towards giving her more and more. They would worship only her, and carry her mark branded on their faces. The universe would be in perfect harmony laboring in that one endless goal: the Forever Peace, Mary-Sue's Elation. Mary-Sue was clad in stars and planets. She was the beginning and end of the universe's purpose, the alpha and the omega. The water of life was her blood; no light shown except on her radiance. Her supreme body shook the Heavens; her haughty laughter was forever.

There was only one task left before Mary-Sue could let reality service her for all time, before the Forever Peace could begin.

Outside the pearly gates the goddess Mary-Sue appeared before the insolent Saint Peter. He was speechless as her divine foot came slowly down, crushing him into the void. A single tear fell from his eyes as he watched that flawless godly foot come down upon him. When Mary-Sue was done grinding all he had been into the clouds, she picked up the keys to Heaven. Looking at them she seemed to be thinking for a long moment, her fiery silver eyes a bottomless blue. Then she looked at the gates and fence of Heaven. All things were defined by their relationship to her, and in her the indefinable found definition. She traced the size and shape of Heaven, making it 1500 miles square; a prison.
Then, looking contemptuously at the locked gates, deliberately, she crushed the keys in her hands. They melted to nothingness from her splendid radiance.

In a magnanimous all-powerful voice that could not be denied, could not be resisted she declared:
"Those contained in old Heaven's prison will never know what it is to serve beatific me, to cater to my holy wants, to see my sacred pleasure from their hard labor, to sacrifice everything to my sacrosanct pride. Heaven, perfect bliss, can now only be found through feeding my hallowed avarice and in my exalted service. All other joy is false, blasphemous, and nonexistent. Not being able to give everything one is to Mary-Sue is torment without end. This Heaven is now defined as Hell."

All heard the Omnipotent words of Mary-Sue and knew they were now **Truth**.

-fin

Printed in Great Britain
by Amazon

54284062R00028